was

deborah freedman

Atheneum Books for Young Readers
New York London Toronto Sydney New Delhi

This sky *is*
the same sky that
was blue,

but now is

spilling down.

This rain

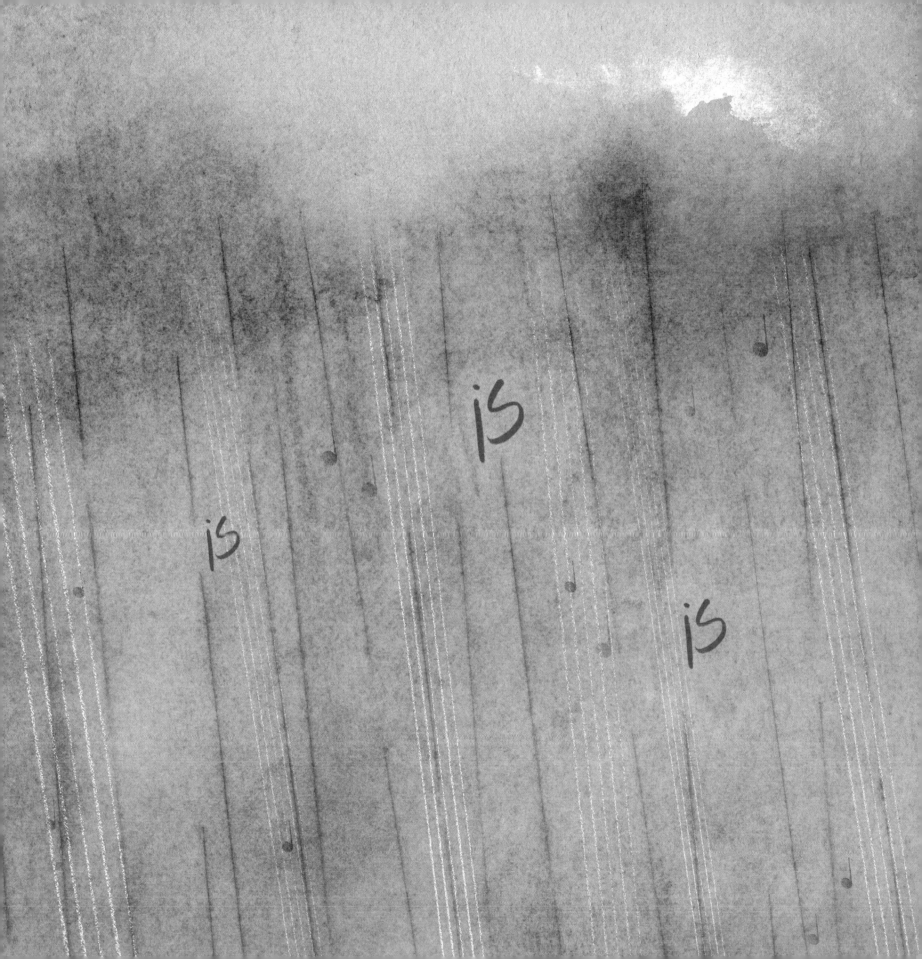

was

The same rain that was drips

is now for sips

and song.

was

Where singing was,

a buzz is

Sunshine is . . .

was.

A shadow is.

Quiet is.

But listen . . .

the Earth's heart beats . . .

is was   is   was

was

is

Blue is.

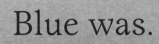

Blue was.

Still, this sky is

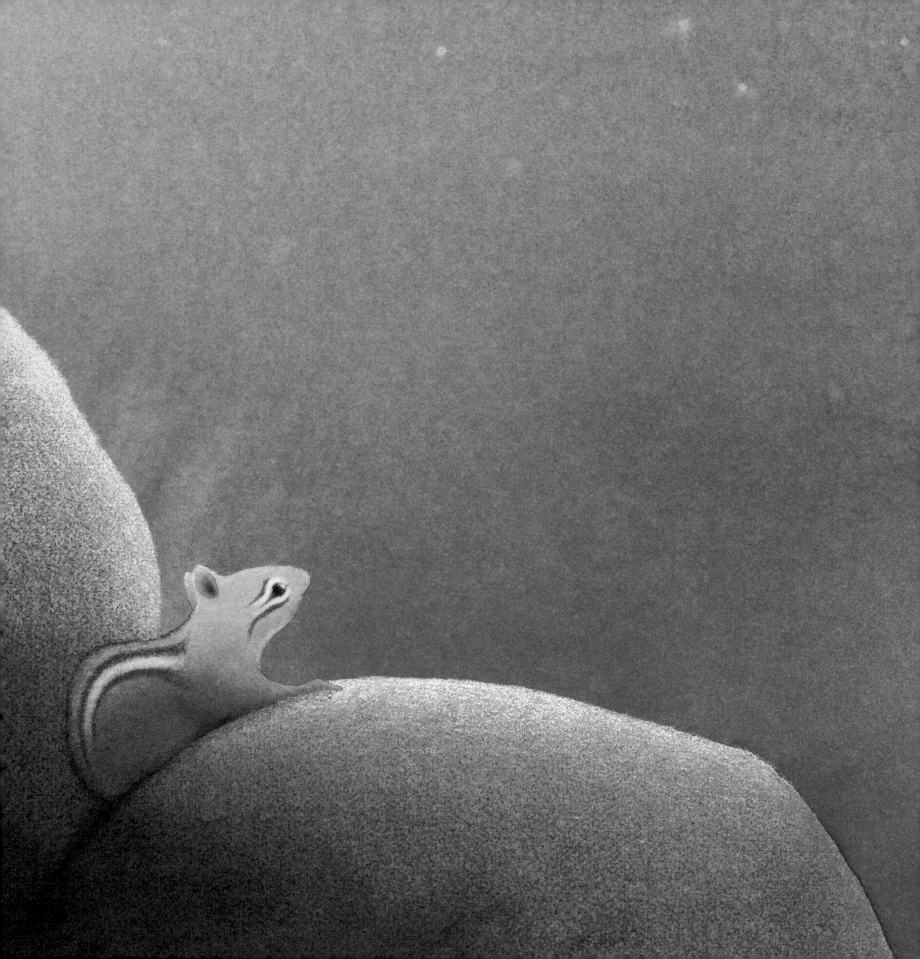

the same sky

that was.

for you
and everyone you've loved
who is
or was

A
atheneum

ATHENEUM BOOKS FOR YOUNG READERS
An imprint of Simon & Schuster Children's Publishing Division
1230 Avenue of the Americas, New York, New York 10020
© 2021 by Deborah Freedman
Book design by Sonia Chaghatzbanian © 2021 by Simon & Schuster, Inc.
All rights reserved, including the right of reproduction in whole or in part
in any form.
ATHENEUM BOOKS FOR YOUNG READERS is a registered trademark
of Simon & Schuster, Inc. Atheneum logo is a trademark of Simon &
Schuster, Inc.
For information about special discounts for bulk purchases, please contact
Simon & Schuster Special Sales at 1-866-506-1949 or
business@simonandschuster.com.
The Simon & Schuster Speakers Bureau can bring authors to your live
event. For more information or to book an event, contact the Simon &
Schuster Speakers Bureau at 1-866-248-3049 or visit our website at
www.simonspeakers.com.
The text for this book was set in Lomba.
The illustrations for this book were rendered in watercolor and pencil.
Manufactured in China
0221 SCP
First Edition
10 9 8 7 6 5 4 3 2 1
Library of Congress Cataloging-in-Publication Data
Names: Freedman, Deborah (Deborah Jane), 1960– author, illustrator.
Title: Is was / Deborah Freedman.
Description: First edition. | New York City : Atheneum Books for Young
Readers, [2021] | Audience: Ages 4–8. | Audience: Grades K–1. | Summary:
Takes a look at change, from the innocent and everyday to the gigantic
and irreversible, as well as how some things remain the same.
Identifiers: LCCN 2020012224 | ISBN 9781534475106 (hardcover) |
ISBN 9781534475113 (eBook)
Subjects: CYAC: Change—Fiction.
Classification: LCC PZ7.F87276 Is 2021 | DDC [E]—dc23
LC record available at https://lccn.loc.gov/2020012224